Moon and Me

The Little Seed

Andrew Davenport
Illustrated by Mariko Umeda

SCHOLASTIC

Special thanks to Avalon Lily Lenz and her parents Caitlyn and Nathan.

Scholastic Children's Books,
Euston House, 24 Eversholt Street,
London NW1 1DB, UK

A division of Scholastic Ltd
London ~ New York ~ Toronto ~ Sydney ~ Auckland
Mexico City ~ New Delhi ~ Hong Kong

Published in the UK by Scholastic Ltd, 2019

ISBN 978 1407 18852 2

Printed and bound in Italy

2 4 6 8 10 9 7 5 3 1

www.scholastic.co.uk

Contents

'Hush, Hush,' Says the Moon…

'It's time to go to sleep.'

Lie down, Pepi Nana.

Close your eyes, don't you peep!

This is the way we go to sleep.

Lie down, Mr Onion…

Colly Wobble…

Sleepy Dibillo…

Little Nana…

Lambkin…

And Lily Plant – some water for you.

Here's something for you
to find when you wake up.
Some coloured tissue paper.

Night, night!

Moon, can we have a story?

'A story,' says the moon.

'What a good idea…'

This is the story of one special night when the
moon was shining brightly.

The story of how Pepi Nana met a new friend, Moon Baby.

One Special Night

Whenever the moon shines on Pepi Nana, she wakes up. She walks and talks and plays. Pepi Nana is a very magical toy indeed.

Look – she's waking up right now.
Hello, Pepi Nana!

'Tiddle toddle!'

Pepi Nana went looking for her friends, but nobody was awake.

So, do you know what Pepi Nana did?

Pepi Nana sat down at her desk with her favourite pencil and wrote a magical letter.

Do you know who to?

To the moon!

It went like this…

Tiddle toddle!
Please come to tea, and we can have a story.
Yours, lovingly out of the window,
Pepi Nana

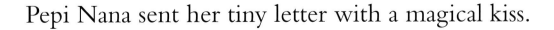

Pepi Nana sent her tiny letter with a magical kiss.

Away went the tiny letter, to the moon.

A Visitor From the Moon

Pepi Nana didn't know that on the moon lived Moon Baby.

Look! Here comes the tiny letter!

Moon Baby had never seen a letter before.
The tiny envelope landed right next to him.

He opened it up.

Tiddle toddle!
Please come to tea, and we can have a story.
Yours, lovingly out of the window,
Pepi Nana

Moon Baby wanted to visit Pepi Nana, very much.

He picked up his magical kalimba, put on his
yellow gloves and pulled up his hood.

He was ready to go.

Moon Baby flew all the way down from the moon.

Look up to the sky, you might see him go by!

Moon Baby landed – bump! – right in front of the Toy House.
He put down his hood and took off his yellow gloves.
He pressed the big toy doorbell.

Ding dong! Ding dong!

Pepi Nana hurried down the stairs to answer the door.

'Tiddle toddle!' she said.
Moon Baby has come to visit!

He blew Pepi Nana a kiss.
'Come in, come in!' said Pepi Nana.

Time for Moon Baby to wake up Pepi Nana's friends.

Moon Baby played his magical kalimba and one by one, the toys woke up.

Pepi Nana was very excited to see her friends.
'Everybody is awake,' she said. 'Thank you, Moon Baby!'

'I Love You' Song

I love you.

More than a sunny day,
More than the Milky Way,
More,
More.

I love you, more,
In every way,
More, than a song can say.

So many stories
Wait for us each day –

Every day
A way to say
'I love you.'

I love you.

Tissue Flowers

Inside the little toy house, everybody was very busy.

'Look what I found in the curiosity box!' said Pepi Nana.
'Tissue paper! I'm going to make something.'

'And me!'

'And me!'

'And me!'

'And me!'

'And me!'

'Tissue flowers are easy to make,' said Pepi Nana.

And I think she was right about that.

Everybody set to work, scrunching and bunching the colourful tissue paper.

But Little Nana found it hard to make a tissue flower. *I'm too little*, she thought.

She scrunched up her paper into a ball. Oh, dear. It didn't look much like a flower.

Little Nana felt sad.

'Poop-poop!'

When everybody had finished their flowers, Pepi Nana asked
Lily Plant to choose which she liked best.

Lily Plant looked at Little Nana's tissue ball.

'Oh, my dears! I like that one best,' she said. 'Because it looks like a seed.'

Little Nana felt happy.

'It's a magical seed,' she said.

And Pepi Nana said, 'What a useful thing for a story!'

Time for Moon Baby to take us to Storyland.

Moon Baby took out his magical
kalimba and played some very
magical music.

The Little Seed

Once upon a time, Little Nana planted her magical seed. Mr Onion watered it.

Moon Baby played magical music, and do you know what happened?

It grew … and it grew … and it grew

'Tiddle toddle!' said Pepi Nana. 'Little Nana's little seed has grown into a very tall beanstalk!'

And I think she was right about that.

'Poop-poop!' said Little Nana. 'Let's climb the beanstalk, to see what's at the top!'

'We always do things together,' said Pepi Nana.

So, up they climbed. Up and up and up – higher and higher and higher, until they reached the very top of the beanstalk.

And what do you think they saw?

It was the most enormous tissue-paper flower you
ever did see.

'You should meet our friend Lily Plant,' said Pepi Nana.

'My dears, I should be delighted!' said the flower.

So, Moon Baby played some very magical music.

And right there beside them in the clouds, their Toy House appeared, and Lily Plant looked out.

Every One is Special

'Oh, my dears!' said Lily Plant. 'How lovely to see you all!'

They talked together for a very long time.
The tissue flower was very happy to see Lily Plant, too.

'What are they talking about?' wondered Little Nana.

'All the things that plants like,' said Mr Onion. 'Sunny days, bees, rain and tablecloths.'

'Tiddle toddle!' said Pepi Nana. 'How lovely that we have a new friend!'

And they all showed their new friend the tissue-paper flowers they had made.

'Every one is special!' said the enormous flower.

And I think she was right about that.

The Friendship Song

Friendship is a seed we sow
Water the seed and watch it grow.

Sometimes fast, sometimes slow
Sometimes it takes time to show.

Water the seed, it won't be long
Friendship will grow tall and strong.

The most important thing I know
Friendship is a seed we sow.

Water the seed
And watch it grow.
Water the seed
And watch it grow.

At last it was time to say
goodbye to their new friend.

'What a very special day
it's been!' said the enormous
flower.

Lily Plant fluttered her petals
and everybody waved their
tissue-paper flowers.

'Goodbye, new friend!'
they all said.

Time for Tea

'Tiddle toddle!' said Pepi Nana.
'What a lovely story of our
lovely new friend!'

'All grown from Little
Nana's little seed!' said
Mr Onion.

And I think he was right about that.

'Tiddle toddle, tiddle toddle!' said Pepi Nana.

'We made a lovely story.'

And everybody thought she was right about that.

'Hush, hush,'
says the moon.
'It's time to go
to sleep.'

40

Close your eyes, don't you peep!
This is the way we go to sleep.

Goodnight, Everybody

Everybody went to find their very own bed.

Goodnight, Dibillo.

Goodnight, Mr Onion.

Goodnight, Lambkin.

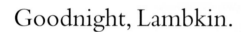

Goodnight, Little Nana.

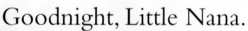

Goodnight,
Colly Wobble.

Goodnight, Lily Plant.

Pepi Nana said goodbye
to Moon Baby.

'Write me another
letter soon!' he said.

Moon Baby took out his magical kalimba
and played magical music.

Then he blew Pepi Nana a kiss.

'Bye-bye, Moon Baby,' said Pepi Nana.

And off he flew, back to the moon.

'Tiddle toddle, tiddle toddle!'

Pepi Nana climbed
the Toy House stairs
to her very own bed.

Pepi Nana pulled the cosy covers up around her.
She laid her head on the pillow and closed her eyes.

'Tiddle toddle!' she said, as she fell asleep.

Goodnight, Pepi Nana.

Goodnight, Moon Baby.

And that is the end of the story.

The End